SCARRY WORD BOOK
My Day

Illustrated by Richard Scarry

Hamlyn

Good Morning!

Here is Bear.
He has just got out of bed.
He washes his face and hands.
He brushes his teeth and combs his hair.
Can you do these things by yourself?

Now Bear gets dressed.
He puts on his yellow shirt
and his red trousers.
Then he makes his bed.
He really is a clever bear!
Now, Bear, hurry to
breakfast.
Soon it will be time for
school.

At School

Big children go to school.
They have their own pencils, pens, and books.
The teacher helps them learn to read and write.
Somebody is writing on the blackboard.
A . . . B . . . C . . .
Do you know your ABC?

Point to:

book   Biro   notebook   fountain pen
pencil   desk   chalk   wastepaper basket
apple   pupil   teacher   blackboard

Art Class

Bear is drawing a picture with some coloured chalk. Penny Pig is painting a picture of some fruit. Look at Squeaky's painting! He has made a very large picture of a very large dinosaur.

Can you find:

apple   crayons
ladder   tube of paint
banana   paintbrush
chalk   paintbox

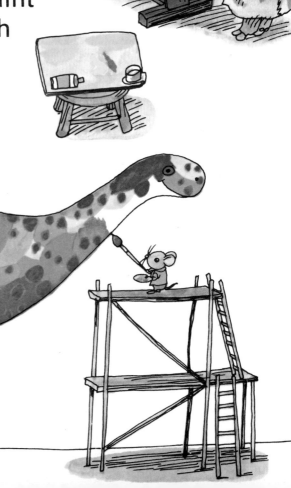

Playtime

School is over.
Bear and his friends go to
the playground.
They like to climb on the
climbing frame.

What do you like to do?

play quoits
blow bubbles
spin on the roundabout
slide down the slide
climb on the climbing frame

11

To Town

On Saturdays, Bear goes
into town with his
mother and father.
They ride on the big red
bus.
Bear likes to go to town,
because there is always
so much to see.

Can you see:

bus	park bench
tree	street
manhole	blue car
pavement	cinema
statue	café
yellow car	flags

Fire! Fire!

One Saturday, Bear saw a
house on fire.
Then Bear heard the fire
brigade coming.
The firemen sprayed water
on the fire.
They rescued Little Cat.
Soon the fire was out.
Good work, firemen!

Point to:

fire extinguisher
fire-engine
fireman
safety net
Bear
hose
ladder
Little Cat

At the Shop

Sometimes, after school, Bear
goes to the shop for his mother.
Today, she wants some lettuce
and tomatoes.
Mrs Pig is buying some
groceries, too.

HAMLYN BOOKS

Can you find:

vegetables

books   purse
bottle of milk   cauliflower
peas   carrots
money   onions

17

At the Doctor's Surgery

Bear's mother is a nurse.
She works for Doctor Lion.
When school is over, Bear goes to meet her
at the doctor's surgery.
Do you see the bandage on Doctor Lion's
tail?
He caught his tail in the door.
OUCH! Bear's mother put some ointment on
the cut and bandaged it.

Can you see:

Bear's mother
Doctor Lion
thermometer
bandage
sticking plaster
scissors
tweezers
scales

19

What did you do today?

jump over
something

crawl under
something

fall down

get up

go to bed

read a book   watch television

dig a hole   play with a ball   write a letter

What do they do all day?

Many people work at a job all day.
Does your mother or father have a job?
Do you know what kind of job it is?

Point to:

butcher
farmer
sailor
nurse
doctor
carpenter
cook
typist